Also by David McKee:
Elmer and Rose
Elmer and Snake
Elmer and Super El
Elmer and the Big Bird
Elmer and the Birthday Quake
Elmer and the Hippos
Elmer and the Rainbow
Elmer's Christmas
Elmer's First Counting Book
Elmer's Opposites
Elmer's Special Day

American edition published in 2013 by Andersen Press USA,
an imprint of Andersen Press Ltd.
www.andersenpressusa.com

First published in Great Britain in 2013 by Andersen Press Ltd.,
20 Vauxhall Bridge Road, London SW1V 2SA.
Published in Australia by Random House Australia Pty.,
Level 3, 100 Pacific Highway, North Sydney, NSW 2060.

Copyright © David McKee, 2013.

All rights reserved. No part of this book may be reproduced, stored in a retrieval system,
or transmitted in any form or by any means—electronic, mechanical, photocopying,
recording, or otherwise—without the prior written permission of Andersen Press Ltd.,
except for the inclusion of brief quotations in an acknowledged review.

Distributed in the United States and Canada by
Lerner Publishing Group, Inc.
241 First Avenue North
Minneapolis, MN 55401 USA
For reading levels and more information, look up this title at www.lernerbooks.com.

Color separated in Switzerland by Photolitho AG, Zürich.
Printed and bound in Malaysia by Tien Wah Press.
David McKee works in gouache and colored pencils.

Library of Congress Cataloging-in-Publication data available.
ISBN: 978–1–4677–3453–0
eBook ISBN: 978–1–4677–3456–1
1 – TWP – 12/1/13

ELMER
and the WHALES

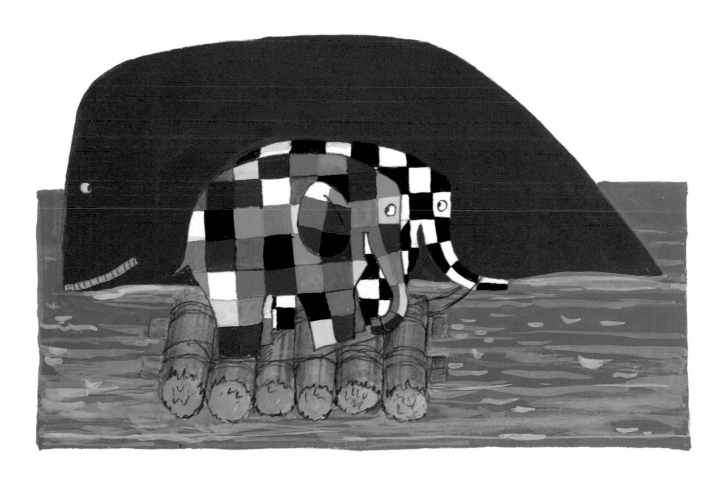

David McKee

Andersen Press USA

Elmer, the patchwork elephant, and his cousin Wilbur were visiting Grandpa Eldo.

"When I was your age," said Grandpa Eldo, "at this time of year, I used to follow the river down to the coast and watch the whales go by."

"Whales? Fantastic!" said Elmer. "Come on, Wilbur, let's go and see them."

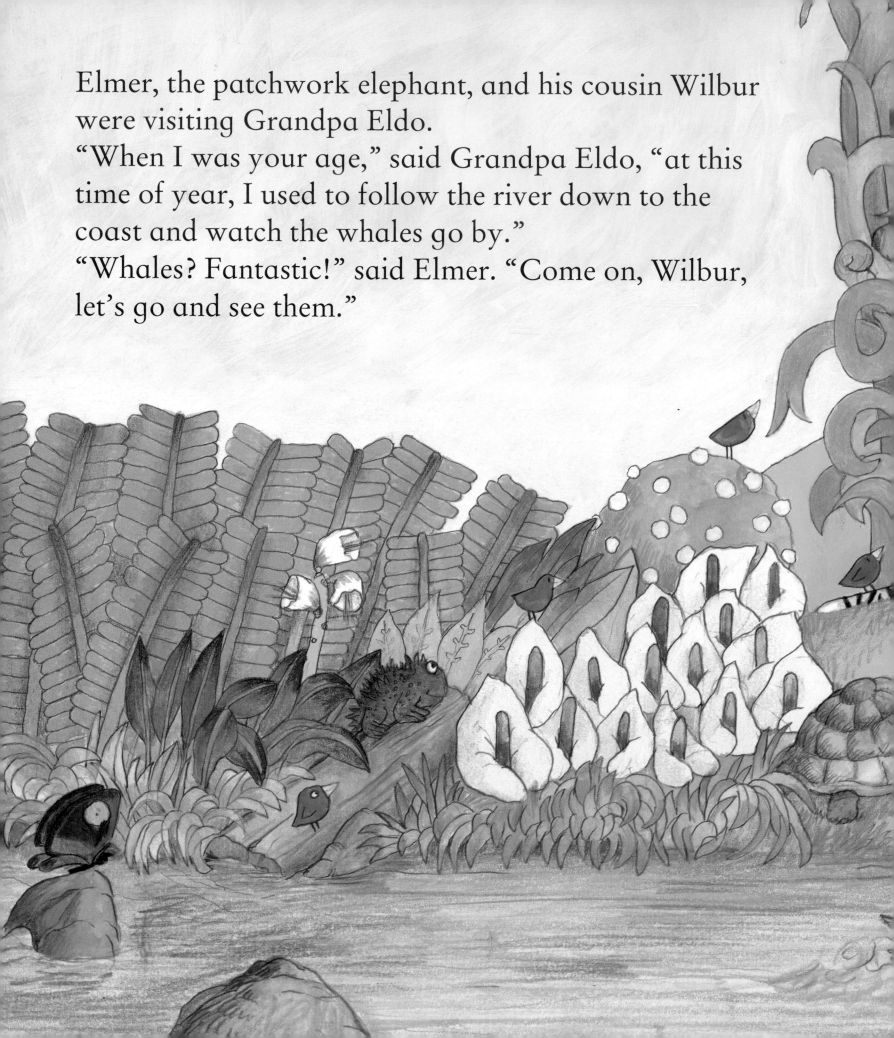

"Come with us, Lion," said Elmer. "You too, Tiger."

"I'd love to, Elmer," said Lion, "but I have a nap that needs finishing."

"Sorry," said Tiger, "I have to be back by teatime, and the sea is a long way away."

"Just follow the river," called Grandpa Eldo.

They hadn't gone far, when they met the crocodiles.
"Hello, Crocodiles," they said. "We're following the river
down to the sea."
"Why follow it?" asked a crocodile. "Make a raft. There
are enough tree trunks lying around."
"We'll help you tie them together," said the monkeys.

The monkeys tied the logs together with
creepers and the raft was soon ready.
The noise attracted the hippos.
They chuckled when they saw what was going on
and gave the elephants a push start.
"Now the river will take you," they said. "Good luck!"

The raft drifted gently through the jungle.
"If you prefer, Wilbur, we can always land and walk,"
said Elmer.

"You must be joking," said Wilbur. "This is easier, and the jungle looks different from here."

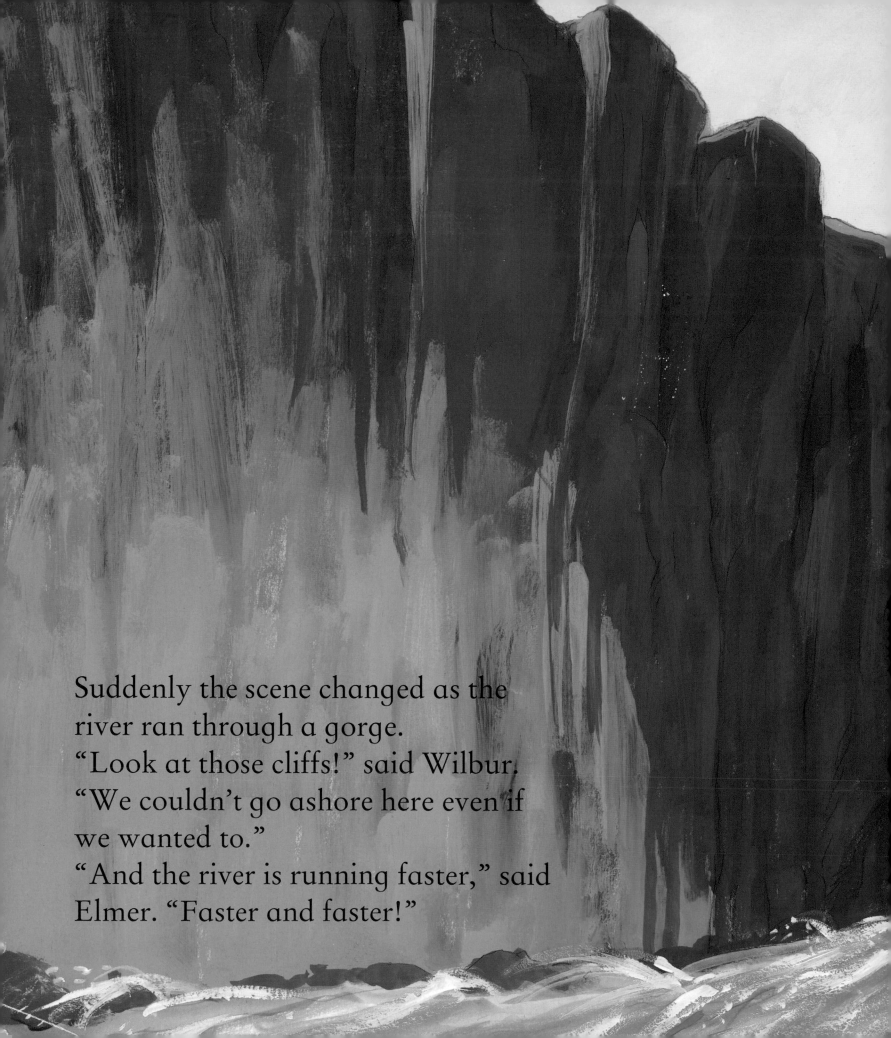

Suddenly the scene changed as the
river ran through a gorge.
"Look at those cliffs!" said Wilbur.
"We couldn't go ashore here even if
we wanted to."
"And the river is running faster," said
Elmer. "Faster and faster!"

"Oh no, rapids!" said Elmer.
The river that had been so gentle, now threw
the raft every which way and the other.
"Hold on, Wilbur!" shouted Elmer.
"Hold on, Elmer!" shouted Wilbur.
"I am!" they both shouted together.

The rapids ended as suddenly as they had started.
"Wow!" Wilbur laughed. "We're still on the raft, but we
still can't land."
"We'll just have to wait until we drift in," said Elmer.
"We're getting closer to the sea. Look at the birds."

By now the cousins were tired from the long, exciting trip.

As night fell, the raft gently rocked them to sleep.

Morning came and they awoke with a start.
"Oh no," said Elmer. "We haven't drifted in,
we've drifted *out*. We're at sea!"
"At sea with the whales," said Wilbur.
"Hello," called Elmer. "Could you push us ashore, please?"

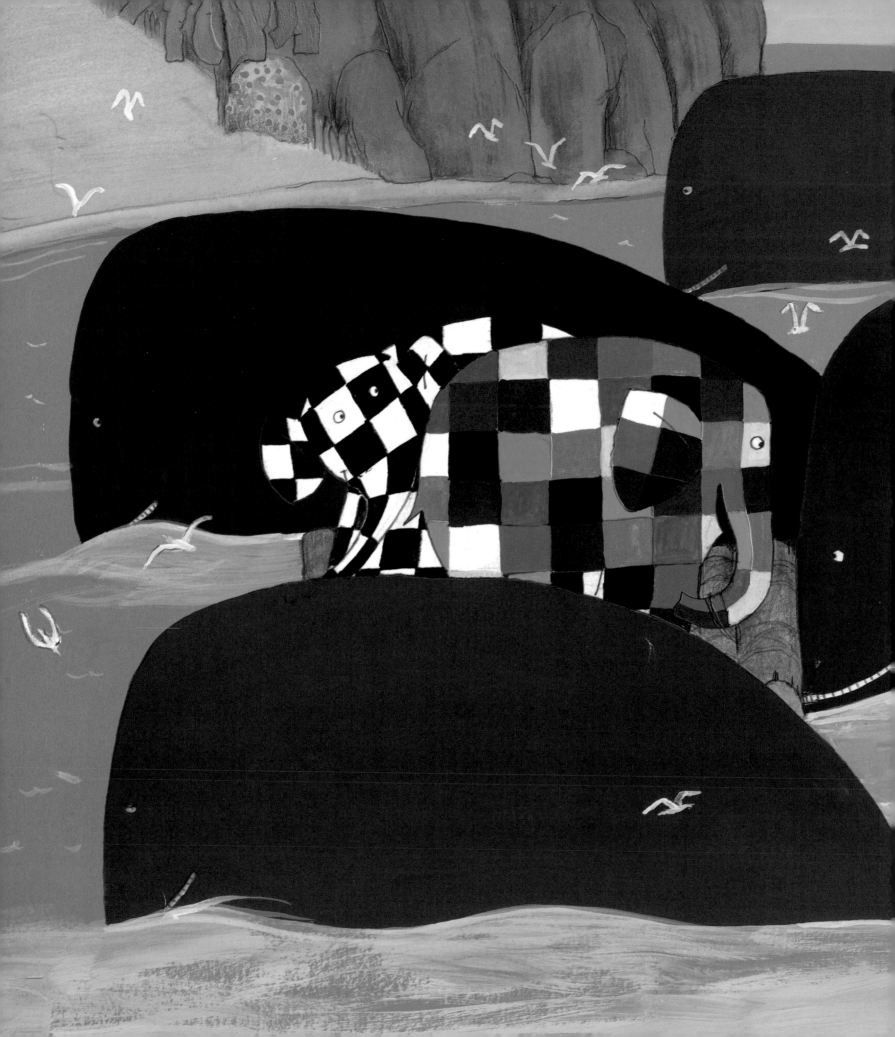

"We came especially to see you," said Elmer. "It's the first
time we've seen whales. It's probably the first time you've
seen an elephant on a raft," he laughed.
"No, it's the second time," said a whale. "When I was
young, a golden one came on a raft."
"Grandpa Eldo!" said Elmer and Wilbur together.

Once ashore, Elmer and Wilbur found a place to watch the whales as they went on their way.
"Say 'Hello' to Eldo from us," called the whales.
"I'll say more than 'Hello'!" muttered Wilbur.
"Yes," said Elmer. "I wonder what other stories he hasn't told us!"